SURVIVING
AN ICE
AGE

MADELINE TYLER

Gareth Stevens
PUBLISHING

Please visit our website, www.garethstevens.com.
For a free color catalog of all our high-quality books, call toll free 1-800-542-2595
or fax 1-877-542-2596.

Cataloging-in-Publication Data

Names: Tyler, Madeline.
Title: Surviving an ice age / Madeline Tyler.
Description: New York : Gareth Stevens Publishing, 2019. | Series: Surviving the impossible |
Includes glossary and index.
Identifiers: ISBN 9781538235188 (pbk.) | ISBN 9781538235201 (library bound) | ISBN
9781538235195 (6pack)
Subjects: LCSH: Glacial epoch--Juvenile literature.
Classification: LCC QE697.T95 2019 | DDC 551.7'92--dc23

First Edition

Published in 2019 by
Gareth Stevens Publishing
111 East 14th Street, Suite 349
New York, NY 10003

© 2019 Booklife Publishing
This edition is published by arrangement with Booklife Publishing

Written by: Madeline Tyler
Edited by: John Wood
Designed by: Danielle Jones

Printed in the United States of America

CPSIA compliance information: Batch #CW19GS. For further information, contact Gareth Stevens, New York, New York at 1-800-542-2595.

CONTENTS

Words that look like THIS can be found in the glossary on page 31.

HERE COMES THE ICE

Have you ever wished that it would snow so that you could get a day off school? Maybe you've got math class tomorrow morning and you haven't done the homework, or you've got a history test that you haven't studied for (again). Or would you just like a day of ice-skating and snowball fights? Well, it may be your lucky day. Temperatures around the world have been falling to record lows and it doesn't look like they're going to get warmer anytime soon. Maybe this is the start of an ice age that could last for thousands, maybe even millions, of years!

Some scientists don't think we're going to enter another ice age for at least another 100,000 years, but others believe that one could start any day now! Even if the ice age doesn't start today, you'll still need to be prepared!

You'll need to learn how to become a survival expert very quickly if you're going to make it through the **SUBZERO** temperatures of an ice age alive. This guide contains everything you'll ever need to know about surviving in an ice-covered wasteland. You'll learn all about finding the perfect shelter, what you can eat when everywhere around you is frozen, and how to stop yourself from freezing to death. You could find yourself in great danger and separated from your friends and family, so it's important that you know how to look after yourself.

THE LAST ICE AGE

Don't worry – this isn't the first ice age, and it won't be the last either. There have already been five major ice ages in the Earth's history, with the most recent one ending around 10,000 years ago. As the world slowly got covered in ice and the climate became cooler, it made life very difficult for both humans and animals. Many small SPECIES of animals died because of the freezing temperatures, while larger animals ADAPTED and grew fur. Scientists believe that the woolly rhinoceros may even have had a special horn for scooping up and removing snow from the ground. Now that would be useful in an ice age survival kit!

Eventually, even the giant, fur-covered animals like woolly mammoths, sabre-toothed cats, and cave bears died out and became EXTINCT. Humans did a better job of surviving, and some historians even believe that we hunted and ate animals like the mammoth so much that we are one of the reasons these animals died out. Many people adapted to their surroundings by learning to build shelters to protect themselves from the cold, while others moved to warmer areas where there was more food available. The biggest problems you'll face during an ice age are the freezing temperatures and extreme weather conditions, so grab your woolly hat and gloves and get ready to battle the cold!

While you're fighting for survival and trying to figure out your next move, it might be a good idea to learn from your ANCESTORS.

EXTREME WEATHER

LOOK UP!

As the temperature gets cooler, clouds will sweep over to cover the whole Earth and you'll quickly be plunged into darkness. The clouds will be so thick that you may not see the sun at all for weeks, months, or even years. They'll bring hailstones the size of golf balls which will make it almost impossible to go outside without taking some head protection or a very strong umbrella. Hailstones can do some serious damage, and some have even been known to break car windows, so be careful out there. If you are brave enough to go outside, make sure you wear a hard hat. These supersized hailstones could easily knock you **UNCONSCIOUS** and you could freeze solid.

Ice

If you can't find a hard hat anywhere, try wearing a bucket on your head. You may look silly but at least you'll be protected!

LOOK DOWN!

When you're trying to stay out of the snow and dodging giant hailstones, remember the biggest problem of all. You're living in the middle of an ice age, and ice ages mean ice! Glaciers are huge sheets of ice that have been formed from many layers of COMPACTED snow. Usually, glaciers are only found near the North Pole and the South Pole, but during an ice age, glaciers move across the world and can spread as far as the US, Peru, the UK, and China. Imagine going to bed one night and waking up to find a glacier outside your bedroom window! This could cause some problems, so it may be a good idea to find somewhere a bit safer and warmer to take cover before the ice age gets any worse.

CHOOSING A SAFE PLACE

As the glaciers move in, it's time for you to move out. Grab your stuff, wrap up warm, and then get out of there fast. Your family might find it difficult to leave all their belongings behind, so you may need to be firm with them. Tell your parents to be brave, leave the TV, and head out into the cold. Make sure your family members are wrapped up warm and are wearing as many sweaters as they can.

Getting around in a blizzard or a hailstorm can be difficult, so everyone will need to stick together. The winds can get very strong, so you'll need to put all your effort into not blowing away. Pair up with a buddy and hold onto each other so that you don't get lost.

JOURNEY TO THE CENTER OF THE EARTH

The first thing you'll need to do is head for the equator. The equator is the imaginary line that goes around the center of the Earth and you'll need to get as close to this line as possible. Countries near the equator receive lots of sunlight and have warm temperatures all year round. However, don't expect heatwaves or sunny beaches – there are very few places on Earth above 32° Fahrenheit (0° Celsius) during an ice age. Temperatures will still be well below freezing and there'll be snow and ice everywhere, but at least you'll be far away from any glaciers and safe from danger, for now…

Equator

GOING UNDERGROUND

Now that you've made it to the equator, it's time to set up a hideout that will be your home for the next few years. It's important to find somewhere that's warm, dry, and protected from the snow and ice. An underground **BUNKER** is a good choice if you can dig through the many feet of ice and snow that have covered the ground. A lot of snow has probably fallen while you've been traveling.

You'll probably be tired after your journey to the equator, but there's no time for sitting around. Everyone needs to grab a shovel and a **PICKAX** and start digging right away. It doesn't matter if Grandma says she's too tired – hand her a shovel and tell her that the bunker needs to be built, and the snow isn't going to wait.

Digging is a great way of keeping warm. If you're still cold, you're not digging hard enough!

You've come too far now to accidentally burn down your shelter. Fire is hard to control, so never try to start one without an adult there.

INTO THE CAVE

If the digging is too difficult, or if you don't like the idea of living underground, you could try to find a mountainside cave that's ready to move into. Bears are known to **HIBERNATE** in caves when it's cold, so triple check that yours is empty before you move in. Caves are usually warm and dry and are sheltered from the wind and snow. If your cave is a bit damp, or if it's too cold, you could light a fire to dry it out and warm it up. Starting a fire in an ice age will be difficult, but you'll need one to stay alive. Collect as much dry wood as you can from around the area – look for trees that have fallen down or any loose branches that can easily be snapped off. Make sure the wood is dry, otherwise it won't burn. You'll need enough wood to keep the fire going for at least a few weeks.

SUPPLIES AND EQUIPMENT

SHOES AND SHOVELS

It will be almost impossible to find any firewood outside while everywhere is still covered in a thick layer of snow and ice. To help you out, you'll need some special snow-clearing tools and equipment that will make the job a lot easier. A snow shovel will let you clear away the snow from your hideout and dig out a pathway.

Before venturing out into the snow, slip on some snowshoes. These will make the long treks to find supplies feel more like an easy Sunday stroll. If you can't get your hands on any snowshoes, you could try to make a pair from some old tennis rackets. They'll work just as well and get you through the snow in no time – just try not to spend too long out there.

Be careful! The ground will still be very icy, so try not to fall over!

LAYER UP

Living through an ice age can be tough. You'll spend most of your time wiping the icicles from your nose and trying to make sure that your mouth doesn't get frozen shut. If you don't want to feel like you've been locked at the bottom of a freezer, you'll need to wrap up warm and layer up. You'll need to cover as much of your body as you can, so scarves, hats, and gloves will be especially useful. Thick, woolly clothes are best, but anything is better than nothing. It's time to dig out the sweater that your Grandma knitted you last winter and finally put it to good use. It might not be your favorite, but it could save your life.

Try to collect as many extra sweaters, coats, and blankets as you can and stash them away in your hideout.

15

Matches

FIRE STARTER

Extra clothes will take the chill off, but a fire is the best way of making sure you don't freeze. Pack plenty of **FIRE STARTERS**, matches, and lots of old books or newspapers to help you start a fire in the cold. Once the ice age takes over, there'll be no electricity, especially not in your underground hideout or your mountainside cave. Keeping a fire going will mean the difference between staying at a comfortable-but-chilly temperature and becoming a human icicle! Not only will you need supplies to start a fire, but to keep it alight as well. Don't worry about fire extinguishers or any safety equipment; if the fire gets out of control, chuck some snow on it and it will be out in no time.

Fire Starters

COOKING UP A STORM

As well as keeping you warm, the fire can also be used to cook food and warm up drinks. The stores will be out of action for thousands of years, so you'll need to make sure you stock your hideout with plenty of food to get you through the long winter. Try to **STOCKPILE** as many cans of food as your arms can carry. Canned food lasts a long time without going bad, so it will hopefully stop you from running out of food too quickly. Don't worry too much if you do run out of cans — we'll get to that later.

If you can't get your hands on any cans, frozen food will do just as well. Store it outside in the snow to keep it fresh.

HUNTING AND GATHERING

If your greedy younger sibling eats all the food in the first week, don't panic. How do you think your ancestors survived the last ice age? Thousands of years ago, there were no supermarkets, no pre-prepared meals, and no cans of food. People had to find and catch their own food to survive. If things get desperate, then you may have to learn a thing or two about FORAGING, hunting, and fishing to make sure your family doesn't go hungry. It's going to be tough out there, but you can't afford to be scared – it's time to explore the wilderness.

Eating plenty of food is one of the best ways to stay warm. If you're still cold, or still hungry, don't be afraid of having five breakfasts, seven lunches, and ten dinners.

FORAGING

The freezing temperatures of an ice age will kill many plants on Earth and make it very difficult for any new ones to grow back for a long, long time. If you're lucky, some plants may survive near the equator and, if you're very lucky, these plants might even have nuts, seeds, and berries growing on them. They may be small and not look like a lot of food, but they'll keep you going until you can get your hands on a larger meal, which could be days away. Try to collect as many as you can and keep them in your shelter until you need them. Foraging can take hours, so try not to lose track of time and get caught out in the cold for too long. It's very important that you make it back before it gets dark – who knows what animals might be lurking in the forest…

Chestnuts

Watch out! Lots of berries are POISONOUS and can make you very ill, so it's always a good idea to take an adult with you if you go foraging.

HUNTING

Eventually, eating just nuts and berries won't be enough, and you'll need more and more food to stay alive. You may have to learn to hunt, just like the people of the last ice age did. They ate lots of meat and animal fat to build up their energy and stay warm. Any spare meat could be stored and kept fresh by freezing it in the snow or drying it out in the wind.

You're going to need to get good at using a bow and arrow if you want to survive the ice age. Try to get as much practice as possible before you go out looking for a meal. You can't afford to miss a shot.

Some animals are more dangerous than others, so always go out hunting in a large group. If you're not careful, you could end up as a tasty snack for a hungry mountain lion.

No part of your catch should go to waste. Once all the meat has either been eaten or stored away, you can use the other parts of the animal to make lots of useful things. Collect the bones to make small tools like knives, **ARROWHEADS**, and spears. These might come in handy later...

Bone Knife

Spear

Arrowheads

Don't get rid of the animal's skin, either. This can be used to make bedding, clothing, and even shoes. These will keep you warm and dry, and hopefully stop you from getting **FROSTBITE**, which could end very badly for you if it's not treated. Just make sure you clean the animal skin thoroughly before you make anything from it!

21

FISHING

If you're lucky, and you've followed all the advice in this book so far, you may survive long enough to finally see the temperatures rise again. The sun will reappear in the sky, grass will begin peeking through the snow, and the ice will start melting. As the ice clears, the rivers will no longer be frozen over, and they should start flowing again. The ice might be melting, but the ice age isn't completely over yet. Luckily, this will give you another source of food: fish! There's no time to be fussy; you still need all the food you can get. It doesn't matter whether you like fish or not – it's time to put those bone spears to good use.

The best place to catch a fish is from above, so try perching on a rock that gives you a good view into the river below. You might have to stand still for a very long time, waiting for something to swim closer. Your spear should be long enough to reach down into the water, but you'll need to be fast.

As soon as a fish sees or feels any movement, it'll disappear, and you'll have to wait even longer before you can dig into your next meal. There'll be no time for arguing with your siblings about who gets to use the spear first. This is no game; it's a matter of survival!

Whatever you do, don't go into the water. It might not be frozen, but it will still be extremely cold.

FROM FREEZING TO FLOODING

As the weather gets warmer and the snow and ice begin to melt, you may notice that there's suddenly a lot more water around. This will cause sea levels to rise, until all the extra water will have nowhere else to go but onto the land. Soon, the coasts will disappear and the rivers will overflow.

Snowshoes won't get you very far anymore and it's probably time to put that snow shovel to one side. Hopefully you packed some rain boots because the water will only get deeper and deeper as more ice melts. Towns, cities, and maybe even whole countries could disappear underwater within a matter of hours.

Before you know it, frozen roads will become rivers and buildings will be 30 feet (10 m) under the water. The only way to get around will be by boat. Floods can be scary, but at least you're a bit warmer now! You stand a better chance of surviving the floods if you stay away from the coast and anywhere else where there are large amounts of water, like rivers and lakes. You could try heading for high ground like mountains, but these come with their own dangers, so bring this guide with you and read very carefully...

Try to find a boat or raft for you and your family to travel around in. Just take one if you have to – the old owners are probably long gone, so they won't mind.

AVALANCHES

As the weather warms up, water will begin to flow down the mountainsides and trickle in between the many layers of snow and ice. Eventually, this will cause the snow and ice on the mountains to melt and break away from the mountainside.

This could come away in small chunks or in huge sheets that hurtle down the slope at up to 80 miles (130 km) per hour, crushing everything in their path. These are called avalanches and they can cause some serious damage, so try your best not to get caught up in one. It could be the last thing you do…

AVALANCHE AREA

Avalanches can pick up speed very quickly and create massive clouds of snow that make it difficult to see even a foot in front of you. You'll need to make your way out of danger quickly, but be careful – every step could send you tumbling down into the icy death trap below. Walk with care and look out for any warning signs like falling rocks. It might also be a good idea to pack your pickax and snow shovel for the trip – you may have to dig yourself free if you take a fall, and this could take hours without the right equipment.

Pickax

MEGATSUNAMIS

You may have survived so far, but the worst is yet to come. Imagine waves that can reach as high as 1,720 feet (524 m) that travel at speeds of well over 60 miles (100 km) per hour, bringing down anything and everything that stands in their way. These might sound more like something from a movie or from your worst nightmare, but they're real. These killer waves are called megatsunamis, and they're usually triggered by a large amount of something – like rocks, land, or **DEBRIS** from an avalanche – suddenly falling into the sea. This causes the water to rush toward the land in a huge wave. If you're lucky, you'll never see a megatsunami wave, but as the ice age makes avalanches and other natural disasters more and more common, your luck may be about to run out.

As huge chunks of ice are dumped into the water below, it might feel like the megatsunami waves will never end. They could go on for weeks or even months, but they'll eventually slow down as the rest of the snow and ice melts and the surrounding earth settles. From your position high up in the mountains, you should be safe from the danger of any incoming waves. If you're still worried, try moving farther up the mountain, always keeping an eye out for avalanches. The snow and ice were only the start of your problems, but if you survived the freezing temperatures and dangerous conditions of an ice age, then you can get through the nightmares and natural disasters that come after.

SURVIVING AN ICE AGE

Ice ages can last for millions of years, so you should probably settle down and get comfortable; you won't be going anywhere for a while. Even after the weather begins to warm up and the snow and ice eventually disappears, you'll have flooding, avalanches, and even megatsunamis to battle through. Life definitely won't be easy, but if you follow this survival guide closely, then you should know everything you'll need to know about surviving an ice age. You'll learn everything from where to go to find warmer temperatures, to what food you'll be living on for the next few months.

The most important thing to remember during an ice age is to stay warm. If you can do this, then you stand a much better chance of surviving whatever comes your way. It'll be a long time before the weather gets back to normal, but now you should be prepared for all stages of an ice age and know exactly what you need to do to survive.

GLOSSARY

ADAPTED	changed over time to suit the environment
ANCESTORS	people from whom one is descended, for example a great-grandparent
ARROWHEADS	wedge-shaped tips fixed to arrows
BUNKER	reinforced underground shelter
COMPACTED	closely packed and dense
DEBRIS	the remains of anything that has been broken down or destroyed
EXTINCT	when a species of animal is no longer alive
FIRE STARTERS	pieces of flammable material used to start a fire
FORAGING	searching for food
FROSTBITE	injury from the cold or frost
HIBERNATE	spend the winter sleeping or in a dormant state
PICKAX	a large, curved tool made from metal used for breaking up rocks or the ground
POISONOUS	dangerous or deadly when eaten
SPECIES	a group of very similar animals or plants that are capable of producing young together
STOCKPILE	save a supply of materials
SUBZERO	less than zero
UNCONSCIOUS	not being aware of your surroundings

INDEX

Photo Credits: Images are courtesy of Shutterstock.com. With thanks to Getty Images, Thinkstock Photo and iStockphoto. Front Cover – Fisher Photostudio, photosoft, Zovteva, frantic00, Quality Master, Lilkin, Avesun, Stone36. 2&3 – stavklem. 4&5 – Esteban De Armas, Koldunov. 6 – By Honymand [CC BY-SA 4.0 (https://creativecommons.org/licenses/by-sa/4.0)], from Wikimedia Commons, Harvepino. 7 – iurii, Warpaint. 8 – lukas_zb, Olaf Naami, rnl. 9 – Yuganov Konstantin, Ksenia Ragozina, By Ittiz [CC BY-SA 3.0 (https://creativecommons.org/licenses/by-sa/3.0)], from Wikimedia Commons. 12&13 – Isabell Schatz, kb-photodesign, file404, Filip Warulik. 10 – maximus19. 11 – komisar, Brian Senic. 12 – bymandesigns, Volodymyr Baleha. 13 – andreiuc88, ra2studio, Vladimir Zhoga. 14 – mexrix , Michael Dechev, marekuliasz. 15 – VladGaviloff, Pakhnyushchy. 16&17 – Mohd KhairilX, Anan Kaewkhammul, Sergey Nemirovsky, yevtushenko serhii, Evlakhov. 18 – Trong Nguyen, David Franaklin. 19 – Alexander Schitschka, slawomir.gawryluk, Vivite. 20 – theSwedishPhotographer, kuruneko, Baranov E. 21 – Vladimir Melnik, Subbotina Anna, Amor Kar, Celiafoto, GoodWin777, Rutalen. 22 – Liliya Kandrashevicha. 23 – Poprotskiy Alexey, VectorPlotnikoff. 24 – Zastolskiy Victor. 25 – Zastolskiy Victor, Thomas Bethge. 26&27 – Smit, Sharon Day, MyImages - Micha, Lysogor Roman. 28 – Amanda Carden, Elena Naylor. 29 – Mikadun, Stanislav Samoylik. 30 – Vixit.